Alfred A. Steele

The Pilgrimage of Light

a poem in three cantos

Alfred A. Steele

The Pilgrimage of Light
a poem in three cantos

ISBN/EAN: 9783337291815

Printed in Europe, USA, Canada, Australia, Japan

Cover: Foto ©Andreas Hilbeck / pixelio.de

More available books at **www.hansebooks.com**

THE

PILGRIMAGE OF LIGHT.

A POEM,

IN THREE CANTOS:

BY

ALFRED A. STELLE.

"Friend and scholar, lover of the right, mine equal kind
  companion ;
I prize indeed thy favor and these sympathies are
  dear ;
Still, if thy heart be little with me, wot thou well
  my brother,
I canvass not the smile of praise, nor dread the powers
  of censure."

—*M. F. Tupper.*

Printed at Meadville, Penn'a.
MDCCCLXXIX.

THE PILGRIMAGE OF LIGHT.

CANTO I.

"*No joy so great but runneth to an end,*
No hap so hard but may in fine amend."
—SOUTHWELL.

I.

In tranquil guise descend unwonted Muse!
  Descend to mould this rude, untutor'd lay :
Soul-warming breath 'mid every line infuse ;
  By Nature's pole star track the untrode way,
  And bid fit strains on man's slow hearing play,
Till heart's deep portals open wide are flung,
  By wild-wreath'd Verse. a guest unus'd to stray,
For minstrel hath safe not recorded sung,
Of age-woven scenes that date these dal'ed woods
    among.

II.

Unask'd I press the poet's wonder-land,
  A mute well-nigh to lore of studied sire,
While at the Muse's touch of stranger wand,
  Outcreeps my immur'd soul of latent fire,
  Whose lazy lines too tardy to inspire,
Accordant join and fill my truant song ;
  That fain secluded would awhile retire,
As o'er life's busy track I haste along,
A crownless child of earth lone melting 'mid the
    throng.

III.

These simple strains I yield to candor'd gaze,
   Joyless save in my natur'd heart alone,
Nor do I strive at wealth of fleeting praise,
   To droop mine homage o'er a lowly throne:
    Such cares mount Fancy's pinions morning flown.
Though charmless in the thrill of metric chime,
   Stirring fled fountain of the spirit's own;
Let me but rouse one pulse in falling rime,
I'll count it triumph then on life's strong march
     sublime!

I.

IIow low the gloomy spirit sinks,
   When cast upon a bed of pain;
And oft the weary sufferer thinks,
   He nevermore may rise again!
How sad, alas! it is when true,
We breathe for such our last adieu,
And take that hand must fall to rest,
For aye across the silent breast,
And hear the closing deep-drawn sigh,
Of fainting nature dully die.
Too manifest in that farewell
To us the tones of belfry knell
That stir the live chords of the soul:
Bid feelings turbulently roll;
Rouse all the pangs of poignant grief, ·
Whose date Ah me! is all too brief!
Those chords though lull'd, breathe oft again,
Of charm hath fled the paths of men;
Of light from out our presence gone,
And shadow left us here alone.
And as upon death's languid verge,
We watch the bea ing spirit su.ge,
The heart frail bends with loaden fears,
Too vast for ministering tears:
Yet when the loyal nigh us stand,
Who glad upbear with willing hand,
To fain allay our keen distress,
Angels of God our steps to bless;

We feel some good may yet remain,
Beyond our nurtur'd task of pain.
But when the last earth-bounden tie,
Low sunder'd at our feet doth lie,
Our anguish burst terrific flows,
And Mourning's direst shapes disclose
Their loath'd habiliments to sight:
We pine amid the wasting night,
And long from earth to soar away
To climes that buoy unclouded day.

II.

Autumn's soft beams refulgence shed,
  Athwart a lowly dwelling's walls,
And clear, as rosy light bespread,
  As pours adown ancestral halls,
Where ice-like idleth sated show ;
  For King of air who thrones the sky,
  On whose high arm all forces lie,
Can nought of sense perverted know.
And as He bade recede His day,
'Mid depths unfound to hide away,
The lustre pale departing, mocks
Bedridden woman's unkempt locks.
It was a wretched place to breathe,
Where Love and her warm care inwreathe,
That had indeed more lonesome grown,
Since son they tended there had gone :
Their only son like shadow cast,
Borne quickly nigh, as fleeting pass'd ;
The sole swift blossom come to blow,
Of wedlock's boughs should hang with snow.

III.

In that south room their eyes grew wet,
  In native warmth but half consol'd ;
Evanish'd he from earth, while yet,
  The violet hid itself a-cold !
And o'er the snows his corse was borne,
Whose crust is melted where they mourn.
They think of him in this still time,

To heaven who trac'd the way sublime,
And while she turns her patient head,
Her consort kneels before the bed,
And yearns he with a dumb-hush'd heart,
For her who from his way must part;
And as his eyes suffuse with tears,
His bosom throbs with darting fears,
And oft he leaves the pallet low,
And stirs with restless stepping slow;
Uncalm'd, uncomforted, unblest,
With soul estrang'd of charm'ed rest,
Not more to dawn till Death shall sever,
To part him from the world forever!

IV.

No creature other lingers nigh,
   To share the griefs of one doth mourn;
Who stranger drops deep-felt from eye,
   Hot tears without the bosom borne,
To weep that spirit press'd to yield,
To nature's warder unreveal'd,
Who guides with zealous fealty slow,
To realms of quiet laid below.
Faint thro' the dank oppress'ed room,
Each object stole a fateful gloom,
Disclosing Want with dark'ning frown,
Had borne his tenants pangless down,
Or led 'long chambers of despair,
With bow'ed weight too hard to bear,
For some cloud-vested in this grief
Do strike at Death to glint relief.

V.

The cares of need by dull degrees,
   Sly crept like thief doth rooms intrude,
And lower'd this meek wife in disease,
   Till nigh the door of death she stood,
To brief unveil the waiting tomb,
Where all must final press for room.
Her thin lips murm'ring strove to speak;
With waning members helpless, weak,

And brought at search fleet store of power,
To lay on wasting converse hour,
While tender light flows out her eyes,
Twin born with Love and with Love dies.
"My husband! hard resign'd thy trust,
I go the way of mortal dust,
Stern-sever'd from thy faithful breast,
To steal from view in hush of rest.
And yet for me 'tis well to die,
And swift in pauseless rapture fly
To realms of glad, deceitless bliss,
Safe from the darkling pangs of this;
Inhabiting where fadeless spring
  Glows ever down the vast domain :
Where worshipers devout that sing,
  Make heaven an universal fane! "

VI.

"With plaint grieve not when I am fled,
  And far from hence my soul be bid,
I number with the countless dead,
  On field and hill forgotten hid.
Ah! well not the memorial tear
To stamp earth-pilgrimage as drear,
Though thou full soon shalt be denied,
Thine own, an outcast from my side.
Mourn not, 'tis but a trifling space,
Till blest we clasp in blest embrace,
Nor led e'er more to rudely part,
With pang that breaks the pliant heart,
The pledges link'd in mystic art ;
For I but fade unbounden'd, free,
When thou shalt come to welcome thee.
Far off remove cold air of Pride's :
Unworthiness alone abides."

VII.

"We will not deign to whisper soft
  Complaint to soil our lips with stain,
For while our higher thoughts, aloft,
  Sky-soar'd above the reach of bane,

Our years have flow'd in blending chime,
As warded 'neath a trustless clime,
And thousands burthen'd with dull cares,
Have wearier urg'd thro' ruder airs.
Vague all to bliss aspiring rise,
No fullness measure to surprise.
Fain would I hark to restive hymn,
As falt'ring sense doth dizzy swim,
Borne chill to Death's unwilling strand,
Whose copse wood veils the mystic land,
Where sky-gemm'd waters intervene,
When deed-lights glad the soul serene.
Breathe wilt thou wonted carol fit,
Till far to bless'ed courts I flit,
As Fancy's melting gleam full oft,
Hath borne my seeming flight aloft,
And seal'd its charm on wilder'd ear,
Till heaven seem'd but a step from here! "

VIII.

Vain effort urg'd awhile to sing,
    The soft psalm of Devotion's breast,
For memories unus'd to spring,
    All shadowy in their dim unrest,
    Uprising, chok'd in harmless raid,
And tears with copious streaming flow,
    Adown his cheeks, nor bidden, stray'd,
    And bow'ed thoughts unwhisp'ring aid,
    Remain'd to grace their natal shade,
Unwont and still unforc'd to glow.
Brief thus in birth-mist wrapt obscure,
    Vain task'd the gift to voice his lay ;
For lo! its melting pathos pure,
Stole on the consort's eager ear,
Vibrating time-still'd raptures here,
    That hours agone light crept away !
And floating far and echoeless,
It weirdly pierc'd the pale recess,
Lone dying, where no arts illume,
Pervading calm of breathless tomb ;

And infinite profound the while,
Death came unwearied in his toil,
And cloth'd in iron-destin'd mien,
So dread yet wondrous to be seen,
Embolden'd led with duteous hand,
The christian to a better land.

HYMN.

I.

The cares, the hopes of life are fled,
 And I shall steal awhile to rest,
In peace that sanctifies the dead,
 And soothes the unforsaken breast.

II.

Unseen I vanish from the sight,
 And meekly trust alone in God
To win me to the fields of light,
 That glad the saint's supreme abode.

III.

Not lightest fears are wont to swell:
 No pallid-mingling dread to die;
There's blessing waits my closing knell;
 That knell, for me the closing eye.

IV.

Methinks in those dim realms I view,
 The wonders of the Holy One,
Whose trackless glories vast pursue,
 From world to world, from sun to sun!

V.

'Tis hour of joy when guest hath come;
 That hour I long have yearn'd to see:
One of the Father's children, home,
 Hastes to divine felicity.

VI.

All hail to thee triumphant Death!
 Thou bear'st me up to brighter skies:
Gladly I yield fatiguing breath,
 To join the blest in Paradise!

IX.

Scarce the faint notes low falling, ceas'd,
When her grace-gladden'd soul releas'd
Sped to those portals oped on high,
Beyond th' remotest reach of sky,
And left in sorrow's dismal mood,
One heart to pine in solitude,
That none do care to foster here,
And nurture with a blended tear.
With dreary pause as one who saw,
O'er heaven a deep-set shadow draw,
And sly on sleeping nature's face,
The gloaming stealthy drift apace,
Till, nurs'd, the vap'rous image bore,
Impenetrable gloom before,
While rude with heavy crushing weight,
He rais'd the loaden chains of fate,
That on him as a canker sate,
And like the forest red man erst,
For whom no sound of welcome burst,
As on he stole from day to day,
Where wilds untravers'd lost their way.
Like as for him come staine'd thought
To close the record of his lot,
But warning high her signals pil'd,
Startling to nature's errant child,
And whisper'd tale of trembling doom,
To those that falsely press the tomb;
Who quench the lamps of being's light,
To which their God alone hath right.
Full over all as seal of breath,
Sage Justice crowns the hour of death;
No mother's heart will quite forsake,
   The lov'd though vile her travail gave;
Our Father, God, can never break,
   Night to his children in the grave !

X

As bend we hastily to clasp,
   From wayside dust beneath our feet,

Some sparkling jewel in our grasp,
   Fortuitous indeed to meet;
We feel to find it idle dross,
The sharp pains of repairless loss.
He stoop'd to kiss the cheek of dust,
Untreasur'd of its angel trust,
Then backward stept as half amaz'd
And down unluster'd features gazed,
With palsied heart, with faithless look,
As if the sight he could not brook,
Though Beauty sate upon her face,
That e'en Death deem'd should hold a place,
Then down her limbs he gently drew,
And clos'd her staring eyelids too,
And with a pang of feebleness,
Vain wrought he labor'd to suppress,
Breath'd dirge-like voice to sore distress,
As ripple trac'd in streamlet grave,
Bursts on the daylight of the wave.
Loveless he turn'd in shroud of gloom,
To life and earth—a spreading tomb,
And read with half unclos'ed eyes,
The loss of all but heavenward ties.
Ah! thus each smile in fortune blest,
Is but a throe to such a breast;
And they 'neath Grief's enchilling shower,
Keen feel at heart the mystic power
Of Love, wing'd breath from boundless blown,
The more we know the more unknown!
O Love and Beauty, sisters twain;
Thou latter if not thriven vain,
In thrall of Praise—disportive chain,
Should parch'ed souls magnetic tend,
   To thy bright tint-pervading shrine,
Perchance, I know not, I may bend
   In flitting homage unto thine!

I

Who doth not pine adown steep vale of life,
   For voice of sympathy to soothing bless;

To cool the fever'd heat of fitful strife,
And list the plaints of eloquent distress,
That, whispering half their tale leave half to guess?
All yield save soulless creature of deform,
Who shuns man's walk-worn haunts, to confess
No kindred ties, and bares the rigor'd storm,
In deep of covert wilds unheeding cit-
ied harm

II

None live so wise to tell the valu'd worth,
Of Friendship's cheer in hunger'd hour of need,
When swarming ills startle in sudden birth,
Where hard walks on through torchless windings
lead,
And as the waif-blown vegetable seed,
Pats lightly on the soil to germinate:
So sympathy on heart's bare waste is spread,
To rootlet nurse, alas! oft-times too late,
To lift the fallen frail or darkling
mask of Fate!

III

Ever on earth-bound thorny pilgrimage,
When tremulous heighten'd ills portentous loom,
May each have waiting angel to assuage,
His ruffled reach to the pacific tomb!
For all may know what life is when its bloom
Fades as the spectre of illusive joys,
Gone on the breath-wind of relentless Doom:
With never, more than mortal sound of voice,
To uprise and glad the heart that recks none
other choice!

IV

And what is charge of earth's supremest boon,
To us vain striving in our frailty low,
But Love's fond aid to displac'd chords attune,
And keep through journey down the night of wo!
Thousands whose dust worn footsteps farther go,
At verging shade would barter all for this:
Or trapp'd in meshy wile for Ruin's throe,
At touch transportant of the fortun'd kiss,
Would love for aye the dame of chaste
embower'ed Bliss!

XI

The time stole on when hands must lay
　Deep hid from Love's caressing sight,
This comely form of fragile clay,
　To slumber out the waiting night,
And with vague memory left enshrin'd,
On dim walls of the perishing mind,
Save of this life—bereavement won,
Whose star is set, whose night begun:
Or how high streams cleft courses vein'd,
In flow unsullied, unprofan'd,
None price for virtue doth remain;
　False light to replace the sun unbeam'd:
Forgiven in unforgotten pain,
　Is all—surviving unredeemed.
Not as the mourning wont to feel,
The long laid grave must e'er reveal,
Lost virtues of the vanish'd dear;
Not so for such must tarry here
No blushless stone to grave her worth,
Will land to those who gaze from earth,
Daughter of duty lived and died,
And heart of broken solace sigh'd,
Nor that late hours half refug'd pass'd,
With hope warm living to the last:
But with Oblivion's trackless flight,
Her worth and name must mantle quite,
And kind Remembrance muse no more,
While Time one gift shall hold in store.
Though borne as bubble on the sea
Of God's diffus'd immensity,
An atom lost in boundless space
Of myriad worlds we cannot trace,
She'll ne'er in fitting realms I ween,
But thro' those courts will find a seat,
In haven of that blest retreat,
Whom like the mighty may in vain,
Desire to grace, desire to gain.

XII.

Of Heavenly Father who can sing,

With fervent soul His highest praise,
Or ever to this low earth bring
  Voice meet to tune celestial lays?
For He our Parent, Teacher, Friend,
Our being's primal source and end,
With marvellous skill and matchless might,
And love and mercy infinite,
Can never mean His creatures ill,
While with an errless order'd will,
Ceaseless He cares for all as one,
Whose steps terrene regardless run,
With Justice holden in His hand,
By Wisdom's self but meetly scann'd.
No mischief higher, minds instill,
Than mingling law with human will;
And let the man who glooms the path,
That seemeth girt by baleful wrath;
Which lingers by the House of Wo,
Where thwarting winds malarious blow,
Forget to murmur or repine
Against the Almighty's love divine,
For aught e'en bids us lightest sigh,
From error opes its subtile eye,
Yet could the vast o'ershadowing,
Of ebon Night's prehensile wing,
Rouse on the vision of the soul,
Like shudd'ring dream of midnight ghoul,
Still should'st thou trust that peace will come
From Death's deep prayerful vigils home,
Affliction how it falls soe'er.
Aside from nature's breed of care;
How long, how oft, though half in curse,
Such is the scheme of universe,
Like virus plant of russet wood,
O'er ill may sapience gather good;
From suffering's furnace all aglow
Angels of mercy tireless go.

XIII.

O'er were the rites, the sleeper lain
  In the hushed grave to grief unknown,

Where Silence sits in steadfast reign,
　O'ermast'ring on her patient throne,
The mourner all unshar'd his tears,
From the lone spot lonely disappears.
Oft when misfortunes crowding throng,
And hearts appall we deem'd were strong;
The vast bewild'ring creep of night
Comes as the withering stealth of blight
And grown a desolating thing,
Dense shade doth on our pathway spring,
Bearing fresh weight to prior sadness,
Till nigh we're steep'd in frenzied madness.
This heart bereft ere matin sun
Day journey hath again begun,
Must quit each fond acquaintant scene
Of memory turf'd forever green,
And with a sorrow-laden'd heart,
Voiceless and voiceless soul'd depart.
The proudest prop to finite ken,
Bears blindness up to all but men.

XIV.

So strong and ardent did he gaze
O'er all with deep dissolving glance,
Where smiling heaven of calm displays,
Thro' the set valley's spread expanse,
And bade each foster'd scene farewell,
In broken tones bare listive fell,
'Mid grief-bent Thought obtrusive come,
Full oft in speechless silence dumb.
"The tendrils of my being twine
Round this home nook like bowering vine:
Where every soft related tie,
Doth knit to earth plaits mellowly,
And where hath no stray'd gleam of thought
Down crumbling Time's chang'd chambers shot,
To mould anew located lot:
But that life might smooth tenor keep
Till Nature hush'd me tired to sleep,
Was all my dream : nor less, nor more.

Ere throng'd at Revery's careless door.
Yet such is fate that oft is hewn.
Rock-path'd a way for us eftsoon,
No seer so bold would deign to find,
Through guardless confidence of mind.
He that decks hall for lightest guest,
Betimes is made the most opprest:
For men in genial sunshine drown'd,
The bard: aside in tears is found.
The patriot breath of freedom'd air,
Stolen thro' vale of bloom so fair
Hath fann'd my cheek for many a year,
By Inspiration's hallow'd cheer
At morn, at noon-tide, even free,
In Labor's spotless livery,
While hope, and joy, and willing care,
Each timid born yet each an heir
Have left with earth effulgent stamp,
From heaven's transfig'ring vestal lamp.
In sainted hours stor'd with the past
That O so fondly look'd their last!
That back can hie to me no more,
On shadowy wing from parted shore,
I watch'd the fields, the dotted hills,
The leafy-shelter'd wood and rills,
When Night slow shut with silence cold,
Each soft in dusk of airy fold,
Wide sprinkling tears that none would say
Were born of pain o'er aught astray.
Oft then my heart hath fill'd with praise,
That thus the substance of my days
Had fallen, like a star employ'd
To fill the waste of teemless void,
And I was happy that the Good
Had plann'd my life to such a mood,
And deign'd to deem me fit to grace
With awkward art the pastoral place."

XV.

"Though mark'd for aye by fate's decree,
  An exile from the scenes I love,

With fancy only left for me,
  Like waif stray blown from bowers above,
To picture memory's tropic isle,
With charms that seasonless beguile,
I could each walk, each well-known haunt.
Long living as a quiet want,
Dismiss without a tear—a sigh,
To trace the graves wherein they lie,
Though all indeed to me had grown,
As sweet well-nigh as poet's own;
Whose birds and brooks, whose skies and trees
O'erflush with tongueless mysteries,
Who doth from close communion draw
Grace, warmth and beauty cloth'd in awe!
But O that mound hard by the grove
Where sober Thought doth tireless rove;
And where though forc'd like slave away,
Still hovers o'er his idol clay,
And close and dear his charge will keep
Till Change shall mock where spirits weep!
Strange stranger under foreign skies,
W'thout e'en the star of prying eyes,
I linger as the laps'd of earth,
O'erlook'd my death, unwomb'd my birth,
Or life would never fix'd me here
'Mong fed things like a desert sere!
I breathe as lone as in that hour,
A western wild-wood mountain flower,
Afar look'd down upon the race,
With many a doubt contentless trace,
But saw and with a mingled joy,
A fairy form my views destroy,
And my proud fabric rear'd on high,
Of cynical philosophy,
Swift totter to its nether wall,
And into thousand fragments fall.
Woman was lifted to the throne,
That fools and idlers shame to own,
For till that star divinely sent

From sky's o'erarching firmament,
Now shining with the glorious blest
Though low her moldering ashes rest.
A creature half of mould divine,
To heal this wither'd lot of mine,
Of truth in woman absolute,
Had oft arisen an infant doubt;
Stood cold, companionless, lip-mute,
To prove at length the problem out."

XVI.

With slow, reluctant tread as tired,
  The mourner trac'd the wild grown yard,
And 'neath a stately elm grey-sir'd,
  Bent o'er the fresh mound prison barr'd
Where lay in dust—it more than seems—
The sleeping idol of his dreams.
No tears from out his eyelids stain
Like prelude drops of hasting rain
That pat upon the turfless ground,
From fresh midsummer skies. No sound
Of sighs, as low breath's sobbing mood
In leafless copse of solitude,
But still, on staying staff he pores
Pale bent, while higher sense than ours,
Sees grief too full to lightly move,
And pities with a gracious love;
But sudden as a bursting flame,
Like asp-leaf shook his palsied frame,
Or as the ague's quaking spell,
Conjur'd by fiend in queasy cell,
Deep o'er his face a pallor spread
Like that which lies upon the dead,
And wrought each feature thin and old,
While down droop'd shoulder ringlets roll'd
Snow-fleck'd, and floating in the light,
Bore full on Pity's leaning sight.

XVII.

Thus bound he lost the pulse of earth,
  Her breathing life, her murmurous stir,

In trace of that departed worth,
  She bent ne'er more to minister
Through little wants as free allow'd,
As to the highest circled proud.

Deeper than lipless Revery's hush
  Of stillness by a moss-grown tomb ;
Softer than wild-rose loit'ring flush,
  In flying season of perfume,
The spell that o'er the old man hung,
Deft drawn in painter's marvellous tongue,
While they low-born discernless creep
Far down from whence the glorious weep;
Who see not where the sacred reign
Of glory falls from chasten'd pain;
Too cold in heart, too cold in brain.

Now half a-stirr'd to outward things
With their dim-fac'd o'ershadowings,
Each sign of grief he doth allay
And hides in chamber cells away,
Then bends afar unfriended eye,
Where distant landscapes lustrous lie,
Which seem to woo with mildest breath
And hint a tale of painless death.

XVIII.

Now one long look around he gave
On all, to carry to the grave,
Like keepsake on the bosom laid,
Thro' all the years of sun and shade
We love to gaze at o'er and o'er,
To bring the light of bless'ed yore,
And ope lost scene or buried thought:
Ah! may such glad poor Childim's lot,
Who turns his step and slow departs
From all once held alliant hearts,
Unpausing down the fruited lane,
At length doth level highway gain,
And views a long reach lonely spread,
As exil'd space beyond the dead,
While deep within his bosom glows

With yearnings for his last repose,
And o'er dejected mind, as clear
As whisper'd sound to passive ear,
While came no marshall'd plaint, no word
Of rude reproach, yet one might heard,
A low suppress'ed sob of sound,
Wherein a melting soul were drown'd :
"Ah me ! these eyes must needs o'erflow,
O'erburden'd with their freight of wo,
Though God's full love abideth still
To bless and guide me where He will !"
Thou mourning soul with sorrow fraught,
A brighter fortune may be wrought
From hope till star of life be set,
Lone lingering and unseen as yet,
Though Nature close her orchestra,
Trust thou that she again will play.

XIX.

But life is life whate'er her dress
Or cloth'd in grief or happiness,
And from the old man's parch'ed lips
Came breath not all of hope's eclipse,
Nor love's; half thought that they once more
Might live and linger as of yore,
Yet much dim fell 'twere vain to ask,
Like musal hum o'er metric task.

I.

"One dropt word to glad my heart,
One warm smile to on me dart,
One soft hand my own to press
Thro' the pale path of distress;
Give me these o'er aught besides,
Life is death where love's denied !

II.

"One long lapse of waveless lull
Over waters beautiful,
That my fragile bark may bear,
Safe down swayless voyage fair,
As to pile of stay'd bank tied;
Life is death where love's denied !

III.

" One ray of hope let linger nigh,
Which rapt vision may descry,
That may I out vague-brow'd night
Haply grope to serene light;
Leave me this my palmless guide.
Life is death where love's denied!"

XX.

Yearnings of soul to such akin,
Dash o'er with wide magnetic sweep
Each dark wave of his heart's ba'sin,
On sylvan fast-cliff lull'd to sleep,
Slipt moment in their chamber'd loft,
By proud aërial breezes soft;
And as the pain of Nature's throe,
Augments to yield an heir of wo,
The tender yearnings felt before,
Dissolve in pangs that o'er and o'er
A-darting quiver through the frame,
Unutterable beyond a name,
Till whelm'ed weakness finds a tongue,
From which the piercing wail is wrung,
That Life doth all at once employ,
To turn to feeble cry of joy,
From travail-vanish'd birth begot;
While flown is all but gift-made lot!
In a less agonizing thrall,
To wanderer thus his doom doth fall,
Heavy like heaven-encircling pall;
And low to Nature half in tears.
He tells the weight that bows his years;
Who soothes with free and generous hand;
A maid that well doth understand.

I.

"My bark bestrides a stirless wave,
While twilight films the face of heaven,
And deep in yon resplendant grave
Glitters hesperian star of even.
Unhued doth Life from cold devotion,
Blind pillow on the bed of ocean.

II.

"I wearied pause with oar delay'd
To dream of when a boy in clover,
Outstretch'd beneath imbrowning shade,
I heard the wild bee hasten over :
Sweet hum that then boyhood delighted ;
'Tis fled : it was not for the blighted !

III.

"There hies a restless beat from far,
As tread of trampling host assembling :
Ah ! doth it seek my fortune's star ?
I wait with reverent fear and trembling.
Gall'd Pride may don her garb unholy ;
Fresh trust enwreathes the meek and lowly.

IV.

"Philosophy smoothe down thy scroll,
And keep each trace by leaflet yellow :
Illume gilt promise of the soul,
No rhyme exists without its fellow ;
Then why should Life her music sever,
Whose chimes ought best flow on forever ?

V.

"The little lifts Hope's clasping vine,
By velvet lawn of wild wood vernal,
Devoid of which her shoots untwine
And fall to trail in dust eternal,
Unwaiting succ'ring dew-drop. golden,
Fit time distill'd though long withholden."

CANTO II.

I.

Staid queen that with meek votary sage dwells,
   And lend'st thy lamp o'er rooms which oft benight,
Wisdom. How dull and pale thy precept tells,
   On listless orb of man's foreshadow'd sight,
   Who longs for, yet will not receive the light,
Till rude Experience comes with stalking air,
   In prism'd letters to red hist'ry write ;
As heaven bestows what earth-clod might not bear:
In clime of truth's essay we breathe her
     fullness there.

II.

Not strange life-step on Fortune's blinded track,
   Unstraying bent thro' swift returning year,
For those aside a deep concern should lack,
   Unread Adversity as cradled here ;
   With soul too wise to shed one kindred tear ;
Whose narrow bounds chain captive prisoner low,
   In dust-stirr'd dungeon cell Sahara sere,
To lose the cup-fill'd blessings that o'erflow,
From life's pure fountain mingling and its
     converse glow.

III.

Such know not earth. They only see the blaze,
   And note the stir of set-selected throng ;
Sky-bubble floats the measure of their days,
   And bears the burden of their deepest song.
   'Tis left for those whose fate hath made them strong,
On fought fields faint beneath a vesper sky,
   To share the heart's hid tale, the slight of wrong ;
Whose breast e'er ready pities with moist eye,
Wide as the wild of pain where fallen
     shadows lie.

I.

There droops a time in human sighs
 No tongue can breath, no charm can reach,
When deep the bedded spirit lies,
 Far down beneath the flow of speech,
While o'er upon the sunny tide,
The graceful minnows moment glide,
Or float along the tranquil wave,
Where sky-blent lillies noon-day lave,
In realm where all is blind to aught,
But sense doth swim in and hath caught.
And as the Pilgrim still press'd on,
With day nigh spent—unnoted gone,
His mind yet linger'd in the shade,
In vain, for feeble cloud-rift stray'd;
When from an old wood's moss-rock'd stile,
Whereon a stranger sat the while,
A voice uprose lightsome and gay,
To him as cold as statue ray.
Adown he lighted from his seat,
Anear, prerogative unmeet,
Like countless those who ruffian urge,
In cloister'd chambers of the breast;
Sacred to enter or emerge,
Alone accordant bidden guest.
A farmer as companion he,
Who bore the old man company,
Or rather lout too slight for tear,
Who dwelt alway in babbler's sphere,
And mindless of apparent pain,
Drove in his prate like driving rain,
Uttering as 'twere by rote, the grave;
A stoice half, and yet a slave.

II.

There scarce be ill so deep and blind,
Falls on life's page to crimson'd blot,
As hapless ignorance of kind,
Unflush'd by man's imperial lot,
But florid grown in pettish prude,
Harsh as in hell's distemper'd mood;

Whose fev'rous fog envelops earth,
Oft issu'd from the family hearth,
Or sunk a-tween the fireside walls,
On circled heart it chilly falls.
The fool (for such are all devoid of sense,)
Like lawyer builds a strong defense,
He thinks upon the treacherous rocks,
Invulnerable to rival shocks;
There weaves the texture of his plea,
With subtlest thread of sophistry.
This scion thus was wont to knit,
His silly crudities of wit,
And garment in the sun he spread ;
The Pilgrim asked to o'er it tread.
Of human nature he was type,
Rough slattern yields with twice-fold gripe,
That graceless did a-romping go,
And forged this imp to grace her throe.
This poetaster—such is he,
With lumin'd gift of minstrelsy,
Like flaming chariot's course is check'd,
That awe-gap'd underlings may inspect,
Or hid like beam of moon's eclipse,
That, bursting gilds a pile of chips.
His was the glory lightly won,
Scourge-mock'd by maxim Solomon,
While he, man-statur'd, infant grown,
Self-worshipt at his being's throne :
Whose writhes of victim, curses seal
Like snake beneath a foeman's heel,
And shorn of Mercy's snowy fleece,
He roams to rob the world of peace,
And worm-ros'd gnaws the flushed mind,
Of odorous hues damask refin'd.
His thorn of easy ugliness,
Belab'ring, goadeth meek distress,
As llama of the bleak Andes,
That lamb-like sinks upon her knees,
To die on Pity's lap caress'd,

And shame tormentor who oppress'd.
He had no heart for others' woes,
Unlike the boor who treads your toes:
Nor deem'd apology were due,
When trampling sacred things that grew,
Till caste hath tent of jeopardy,
To hem the fading of her eye;
'Tis then while servile spirit bends,
By rescuing self to make amends.
Excuse grows thick as summer flies,
That, swarming from the wayside rise.
And finds in lucid explanation,
    A panacea for all smarts;
Excuse had fitly hush'd creation,
    And veil'd the vista of our hearts.

III.

They shortly reach'd a smiling plain,
    Where homes of thrifty husbandmen.
Dotted the fields as ships the main,
    Or nestled'slopes of cosy glen,
They met the view on every hand,
The peace-crown'd bulwarks of the land,
Ere long they pass'd a village green,
Where romping children thick were seen,
Who paus'd with smile in curtsey'd bow,
A mock obeisance to allow,
Most like the bumpkin who took grant.
With Pilgrim like a sycophant.
An inn beside the common stood;
    Paintless its weather-temper'd boards,
As half had lost solicitude,
    For those red-fac'd who lounge in hordes,
Through fell despair it sought decay,
To steal with matron Earth away,
Who doth not know to rob by art,
The gift of mind, the grace of heart.
A creaky sign-board swung before
The red-brick'd archway of the door,
And in a tone light audible,

As changed its shifting letters fell.
It seem'd beseechingly to call
On those who wish to squander all ;
Which secret held a charm denied,
For him who kept the old man's side,
Who thought, while yet he wistful grew,
"I fain would enter but for you
And take my custom'd glass of grog."
Indeed! like any other hog.
A little farther down the road,
The twain in fitting quiet strode,
And left behind the human hum,
That ofttimes seemeth martyrdom
To musing souls that love to steal,
'Neath covert bowers to think and feel.
Hard by the hamlet skirts, beyond,
The waters of a limpid pond,
Reflected Daylight's virgin face,
With more than artist hand of grace.
A herd of kine color'd the flood,
And stirr'd the depths of weeded mud,
Or tranquil, save their lashings, chew'd
With air of mild content the cud.
A score of geese with gabble loud,
Upon the ample pond breast crowd,
While one lone swan with graceful neck,
Where dancing leaves the wavelets fleck,
Glides stilly on until she fades
Beneath the matted cypress shades.

IV.

A fane in mantled ivy crown'd,
   Ahead, of steps perhaps a score,
Where vines together matted wound,
   That wall and moulder'd turret bore,
With peeping eye the Pilgrim sees,
Faint through a tuft of forest trees;
And as their presence closer bears,
They catch the stir of vagrant airs,
That to declining afternoon,

Articulate lisp confiding tune,
As heedlessly they wind about,
And chase each other in and out,
Each crannied nook, each leaflet woof,
And sportive gambol o'er the roof,
Till all at once as stol'n away,
They pierce the mullion casement grey,
And up the rude, dim lighted aisle,
Whisp'ring unworshipful they file.
They lightsome touch the organ's keys,
To faintly breathe its melodies,
That sacred veils its lyric heart
   To beat the choral strains of heaven,
At Sabbath service set apart,
   Or Wednesday's vesper hour of seven.
Along the room each breeze breath flies,
Excepting but the galleries,
Where sighing youth admires the curls
That flaunt upon the heads of girls.
Through thick wall'd-crevice plung'd they
     'scape,
Lute-lost, meanwhile is lost their shape;
Like fairy form in dingled dells,
Their haunting charm cold Reason knells.
        V.
Two poplars by the gateway grew,
   And, wav'd aloft like sable plumes,
Their thin and lengthen'd shadows threw,
   Soft shimmering o'er the mottled tombs,
The graves of many a sleeper lay,
In custom of an earlier day,
Beside the walk, the chapel door,
And 'neath the pointed gable hoar,
While dotting all the fresh greensward,
They lie far o'er the alder'd yard.
The few among the paupers class'd,
In charity who breath'd their last,
Had raised weed mound without a stone,
All cluster'd by themselves alone,

And thick o'erspread by hazel copse,
Where Sundays, some discours'd of crops,
Or gossip'd o'er the latest news,
Or neighbor's troubles to abuse ;
More world-grown 'mid their lowly cares,
Than those who mingled in the prayers.
Now summon'd well each very word,
Committed that our dunce had heard,
"This," said he with a bumpkin leer.
That tore Romance of magic clear,
"This is the frail memorial plac'd
For one, a Bard whose lines have grac'd
The hearts and hands his meed have trac'd,"
As, pointing to a marble vase,
With writing on its snowy face,
The Pilgrim's curious eye he led,
To one lone hermit grave that spread,
To gentle souls in spot unmeet,
For profane dust of roadside feet.

VI.

"In yonder cot," the swain pursu'd,
   "That skirts the hill before our gaze,
This Bard of chosen solitude,
In birth-ray clasp'd his blighted days!
His folk were of that simple kind,
In real life stubborn action find,
Who look'd upon their gifted boy
With all a parent's sad employ,
Unblest of heaven to divine,
A soul of this gross earth too fine,
Who oft with kind endeavor fraught,
And much too oft by rigor sought,
To mould him in the path they stood,
To earn a modest livelihood,
But while his heart was fill'd with love,
Which love could like a torrent move,
The force of nature was too strong,
And bore him in her tide along,
O'er untill'd heath or forest glade;

Thro' twilight church in chestnut shade;
O'er hill and dale and marshy swamp,
With step too grave for frolic romp,
Yet thus he would not seem'd more mad,
To those whose fostering care he had;
He stole to muse with gentle heart,
And ply the magic of his art.
The villagers with looks askance
Of side averted countenance,
Oft shook their heads with wisdom grave,
Reproachful he should so behave;
In an ill-omen'd augury,
He so good so perverse should be."

VII.

" They whisper'd tale though slow begun
   That warm he lov'd a maiden gay,
That scorn'd him for a butcher's son,
   Who wedded her on market day,
And that in after hours, while still
He trudg'd o'er fallow field and hill,
He ofttimes starting came across,
By some fair bank of flower and moss,
Her flaxen-headed little ones,
In summer where the brooklet runs.
That kindly o'er their play he bent,
And lost himself in their intent,
Till, stealing their affections quite,
By share of innocent delight,
Their eyes grew moist to see him go,
Like one we ne'er again may know.
Ere this, his heart grew cold 'tis said ;
He spurn'd the sex and wished them dead,
But doubtless this is word of ill,
Whose fable cup doth never fill ;
Yet well 'tis known Love cross'd his lot :
He breath'd her name but won her not."

VIII.

"How strange, oft dark our spirit grope,
When one alone cell'd bliss can ope,

While others mute our footsteps crowd,
By potent fascination bow'd.
More than bereft because unseen,
They melt in their inglorious mien.
Those most who like the Bard do dwell,
Bid most to breathe a last farewell.
Their thought if come 'tis from the dead
  Of Flattery's praise that deck'd our yore;
For they are never cherish'ed
  As bosom charms of memory's store.
Thus man doth preach affinity,
And woman in a less degree :
Thus was the Bard benighted here,
Like æeronaut in atmosphere,
Where naught but clouds their region fly;
Obscur'd the earth, obscur'd the sky,
And wails his fate as one who draws,
No charm of hope to gild his cause.
His luster'd cheek grew pale and thin,
As like a nurs'd foe dwelt within.
He wander'd by the skirted wold,
Absent as Night 'gan to enfold,
To her dim-shadow'd, dusky breast,
All that delighas to lap in rest;
Nor heedeth he the strokes that fail,
Of woodman on the breezy gale,
Who bends with joke-delighted ear,
A tale of love confess'd to hear,
And steal possession that less pure,
Less sacred held might close immure.''
''O wither'd heart what shall I say
To thy dumb pulse's idle play,
That mingles with the throb of time,
Conceal'd deep silent like as crime,
That sits upon the stain'ed heart,
To never, never more depart?
It asks dear maid that thou be kind,
Though but an humble place it find,
Beside thine heart whose story told,

Would love's divinity unfold:
That yet amid its foster'd care,
To answer somehow doth forbear;
But lingers long, and cold, and still,
   Far as in solitary zone,
That, flutt'ring meeteth thrill for thrill,
   And yet will not receive its own!
What shall I say, or whither turn?
Shall Faith's high altar incense burn,
To purify the hour that may
Outflame to herald golden day?"

IX.

"As wild blue violet twice blown,
   Low hid 'neath droop'd protecting leaf,
Awaiting death in winter's moan,
   Full ripe like barn-loft waiting sheaf;
He dreampt love's dream but once again,
Then too alas! 'twas dreampt in vain!
His heart recess'd in her lone tower,
Where thorn and ashy weed embower,
Where circled row of massy bars,
Shut out the ray of sun and stars,
From his secluded height bereft,
Of balm there was but little left.
The strongest in such hour as this,
The simple right are wont to miss,
Who clasp the pulse of fever'd charm,
That plies fell task of rooted harm;
Which e'en upon the joyous breast,
Doth fill it with a strange unrest.
Such lives that err stern falter'd, though
They bear with more than we can know,
Man's rigid swung philosophy,
Flies at them and it bid them fly,
   hen method chang'd to fitting form,
Persuasive rather than in storm,
Like that for children who are ill,
That cordials take against the will;
Mild pellets for the brother's throat,
Would clear him of distemper'd mote."

X.

"'Twas night, the sable night of years,
 And Passion with her vicious brood,
Had left the Bard to steep his tears,
 In wild of midnight solitude!
'Twas when least tone from woman's lips,
 Were worth the serried hosts of heaven,
That had not known the cold eclipse,
 To plighted troth or honor given.
'Twas in that hour when upward rolls,
The pictur'd curtain of our souls,
And we alone theatric stand,
O'er threshold of the spirit land,
And view dark scenes that awful rise,
To horrify repentant eyes,
When we would gladly give up all
 We have been, are, or hope to be,
Or e'er could to our portion fall,
 For but one gleam of purity;
When doubt dense bears across the mind,
Like black clouds driven by the wind;
When sense and soul are most acute,
And linger half distorted, mute,
Like ear side bent with studious care
To catch the beating of the air:—
Then came a voice that seem'd to woo
Rapt-ton'd, and yet 'twas mortal too.
It led the Bard from his high tower,
Amid fresh dews of summer hour,
Where nought but deep of shadow lies,
Mind-couch'd in woody phantasies,
Yet where in Fancy's tale doth swarm,
All multitudinous in form,
The varied shapes of creature life,
As foliage sinless and as rife.
It paus'd, 'twas gone, the robe of white,
Ghost-vanish'd in the distant night.
He call'd, but vain as mourner bow'd
Who calls to friend that decks a shroud.
Alas! for him whose dream is fled,

He lives, a tenant with the dead,
The Bard doth quake with limbs a-cold;
He bends decrepit like the old,
And seeks again that solemn tower
Whose hold is dark for natural flower.
He clasps his heart to dull Decay,
And Impulse slowly melts away.
O world so deaf to plaintive sound;
 So blind to tragedy of sight:
Lo! prayerful multitudes sink, drown'd
 In the great sea of flooding light!"

XI.

Who deems but Feeling's curious mould,
 For food may languish like the frame,
And left in Hunger's barren cold,
 Slow lose its substance and its name?
Thus heart's fate-bound on pulseless boughs,
By cruel breeze-forgetful vows,
Apparell'd trim in tinted guise,
 Down drop like fall leaf, and are still,
Waiting compassion'd paradise
 To pity and each void to fill!
"This is the frail memorial, plac'd
For one a Bard, whose lines have grac'd,
The hearts and hands his meed have trac'd,"
Rung in the old man's sensuous ear,
And told that some still held him dear;
As o'er the frail enclosure, made
By twisted boughs of circling shade,
The Pilgrim leans with offering sigh,
That might not reach the stranger nigh,
And reads with gaze where moist doth dawn,
The tribute to the poet gone.

THE POET'S REST.

I.

Bow thee low with moist-fill'd eyes,
And meet heart to symbathize :
Under this sod a poet lies !

II.

Hush'd he filleth gentle rest,
With mute hands across his breast,
Oblivious of a life distress'd.

III.

Ill doth soar above him now ;
Wrinkles not his laurell'd brow :
Ah! blest is he far more than thou.—

IV.

Child of sin in frailty bound,
Far from concord's dulcet sound,
Where dwelt in grave hath silence found !

V.

Once unseen his pathway led,
Nows is praise by thousands said,
While birds sing ditty, " he is dead !"

VI.

Drop my friend a heartfelt tear,
For the one, that, slumb'rous here,
Hath reapt too late affection's cheer.

VII.

Long he mus'd with spirit lone.
Ere clos'd hours to far were flown,
Like stem-snapp'd rosebud but half blown.

VIII.

Light, and love, and peace are seen,
Steadfast in their guerdon mien,
And bless the lives that walk a-tween.

IX.

Cold he shivers in the gleam,
That doth a sav'd curse beseem,
And trappean earth a weary dream!

X.

" Why doth Night upon me fall,
Like the dark folds of a pall,
And bind me moveless in her thrall ?"

XI.

Thus in quest he inly strives,
With that Power whose good survives,
Link'd with us and beyond our lives.

XII.

Then his bosom calmer fill'd,
With peace-dews by heaven distill'd,
Whose balm wiled Error never kill'd.

XIII.

Rest thee poet with thy lot;
Myriads treasure store of thought,
From lessons glad that thou hast taught.

XIV.

Meekly from thy earthy cell,
Bide the space whose tramp will tell
For thee, veil'd one, that all is well!

XV.

Matin larks will haste with spring,
O'er thy couch to poise and sing,
Or blithely turn with lusty wing.

XVI.

Draw thee nigher reverent friend ;
By the tomb in muteness bend :
Here all that's mortal hath its end!

XVII.

Bow thee low with moist-fill'd eyes,
And meet heart to sympathize :
Under this sod a poet lies!

XII.

They passed the spot where Genius lay,
And where like sage from classic sky,

The Pilgrim sacred bore away,
  A chalice-reliqued memory.
He could not but dissolve his mind.
With one like him bereft of kind.
Bereft of being's answering tone,
That none could understand to own.
Their feet press on as zephyrs play
Upon the death-lit face of Day,
And steal adown the churchyard wild,
Like mother o'er her slumbering child
That through long hours the nursery beat,
With patter of unwearied feet.
As o'er his couch she bendeth now,
With dear hand on his fever'd brow,
Spoke swain : "The Bard whose lines excel,
  The fustian upstarts bolden'd rhymes.
As heaven, earth with all her crimes,
  Know thou that I can do as well,
You'd scarcely thought that one like me,
Had for a nurse sweet Poesy.
In length six feet from heel to crown,
I'll wager not a soul in town,
Can run as swift, or eat as fast,
Or jump as far without the cast,
Or drink the cider that I can,
On any honest umpir'd plan."
He then forth springs his rhym'd examples,
As merchants do their clothing samples ;
With verses on the birken tree,
Or love, or spring, or misery ;
Which themes are handled with such art
That bids (in vain) the tear to start,
And fills the Pilgrim with alarm,
At prospect of a foray'd harm,
From Nature or her countless brood,
Who venge in more than angry mood,
The mischief'd slanders that they trace,
Done to her by the human race.

XIII.

The ring-bard swain like gateman stood,
By stagnant pool's outcreeping flood,
That long hath nested slime submerged,
Ill lingered and half illy urged.
At length full over was the flow
(For things must have a stop, you know,)
Of his self-arrant jingled talk,
That Inspiration bore a shock,
As still-born, gaping wide her tomb,
Gave all her kindred plenteous room.
He left unsaid until the last,
As though it might be lightly pass'd,
Of aught he knew the Bard had writ,
In roving leisure's frenzied fit.
"One only poem's left." said he,
"Of all his nursling progeny ;
Told oft, but when I fond insist,
To those who then but idly list.
—'Tis this," he spoke with happy sigh,—
Above ths cricket's mated cry,
And mottled owlet's, brood unflown,
In height of windy, wood-top lone.
Way sweet to right ones doth belong,
Whose griefs are borne away in song.

THE LEGEND OF THE CAMP.

I.

"A tale I'll tell o'er the hearthstone bright,
   Of the sunken years agone,
Ere dropp'd on a race the dews of blight,
Or lost in grief was each natal right
   That the pale face trampled on.

II.

"A bright eyed maid of her dusky line,
   Once dwelt in these solitudes,
Before the beam of the heartless shine,
That coldly poureth from Fashion's shrine
   Was seen in their western woods.

III.

"Her sire was chief, but vanish'd each trace,
   That roam'ed his people these hills;
They were indeed a primeval race,
Bound-up in war, who lived by the chase,
   And drank from the sparkling rills.

IV.

"Among the maidens a lovely maid,
   Stood this dark hair'd Indian girl,
Who chose for beauty but nature's aid,
And dazzled in artless grace array'd,
   Unknown to powder or curl.

V.

"Slender and tall with a comely air,
   And manners above her kind,
She fill'd her sphere with a sweetness rare,
Most like as angel were brooding there,
   And wisely through God design'd.

VI.

"Her love was sought by many a brave,
   Of hardy or tender years,
And many the foe dropt in his grave,

To prove the strength of an arm to save,
  In a time of strife and fears.

VII.

"But she was plighted to warrior young,
  And other wooing was vain,
And while in camp was the war-hymn sung,
They felt o'er tremulous heart-chords flung,
  The weight of love's mystical chain.

VIII.

"And stole they oft from their fires away,
  In the tranquil moonlit hour,
To sit where the wafted breezes play
Through wild-wood tree-tops mossy and gray,
  With a spell of soothing power.

IX.

"With clasp'ed hands sat they side by side,
  While the dark pine made his moan,
And sombrous his murmurs came and died,
As mused the lovers in bashful pride,
  Feeling the music their own.

X.

"Strange youth for a savage fiend of war,
  Or a forest maid to love;
Less bold than each of his rivals far,
Who fain in their jealous grief would mar,
  This life with its stars above.

XI.

"But he was kind to women who wrought
  At their tasks with weary heart,
And feelingly marked their cheerless lot,
While, daring scorn and villainous thought,
  Of their burdens bore a part.

XII.

"He in the chase was lightsome and fleet,
  As a brooklet bounding doe,
That, leaving the pastured hillside sweet,
Ere can the eye and the senses meet,
  Leaps down o'er the vale below.

XIII.

"Among the rivals a moody one
  With a breast of crafty hate,
Plotted and brooded from sun to sun,
How Murder might at his bidding, run
  Unblamed for the lover's fate.

XIV.

"Twas wrought at length by his busy brain
  In a purpose dark and fell,
As e'er was nurtur'd by villain train,
The bloody fruits whose innocent pain,
  We shudder as we tell.

XV.

"One morn in the chase's ardor high,
  When many a brave was fired,
An arrow stray'd in its passage by,
And lo! the lover with hapless sigh,
  Down sunken in gore expir'd.

XVI.

"And to a lodge was he silent borne,
  In his night of sleep profound,
While the young maid's breast with grief
    was torn,
For whom alas! she must vainly mourn,
  In the "happy hunting ground."

XVII.

"And just as the dews began to fall
  On the face of mother earth,
They laid him safe from the fetter'd thrall,
That darkly hangeth cloud o'er us all,
  Who wake to a mortal birth.

XVIII.

"Upon a knoll of the forest deeps,
  They buried away their dead,
Where the turbid Cussewago creeps,
And the thick wood now in softness sleeps,
  With its canopy o'erhead.

XIX.

"And oft was the pensive maiden seen,

In the death-like hush of night,
Bent by the spot with a stricken mien,
And o'er the grave would she fondly lean,
　　Till the dawn of distant light.

XX.

"Ah! bitter those tears that steep'd his tomb,
　　Of the mourner lone and sad,
At death of hope in its vernal bloom,
And with vague faith o'er the common doom,
　　In a morn of triumph glad!

XXI.

"She fed on grief and its burden bore;
　　Her face grew meagre and thin:
One eve on his grave her soul pass'd o'er;
The guard of heaven had oped its door,
　　And Death had taken her in.

XXII.

"For ages dim sires rehears'd the tale,
　　With looks of marvellous awe,
And said as the night 'gan slow to fail,
There stood o'er the grave a maiden pale,
　　And startled the braves that saw.

XXIII.

"But all is dust, and Oblivion's shroud
　　Vain mocketh the eyes would weep;
'Tis thus the love of the meek and proud,
In cold, staid lowliness must be bow'd,
　　To the same forgotten sleep!"

XIV.

As pedler with a trinket pack
Prodigious, swung upon his back,
Which quick he rudely drops before
The viny porch of farm house door,
Where all the family hold a seat
From swelter of the noonday heat,
The speaker with relieving sigh,
　　Let go the burden of his care,
But stopped in dull monotony,
　　Nor cried the virtues of his ware.
Without of farewell or ado,

He turn'd him from the highway view,
And through his clumsy cottage gate,
Forsook the old man desolate.
This mental feast he gave, instead
Of supper and a quiet bed.
Such showed the skill to judge of kind,
More stupid, vain the search to find ;
A man he was, for ill or worse,
As such, whom all delight to curse.
For lover well his mistress gleams,
    No dash-light from her tranquil eye,
But love's sound warmth ennatural beams,
    Artless of skill to glance a sigh.
Thus well for him who felt the wrong,
The hurt, that, cloth'd with mastery strong,
He held in check the glowing fire
Of need despised—of arrant ire,
And in the weakness that cannot,
Raise hand to aid a troubled lot,
Tears to his fring'ed eyelids spring,
Swart pain alone remembering,
And course adown their heart-worn track,
Till fondling Pity up looks back.
All have, if one uncloister'd live,
Something to cancel and forgive.

XV.

Like one of old in Bible time,
    Was sorely tried this saint of God,
As fetterless with march sublime,
    To bless'ed land his footsteps trode ;
For seen thro' vision's tissue coils,
Was vexless rest for all his toils.
Poor soul a-weary of the dust,
    From this base earth up-sprinkling showers ;
    Didst know that hallow'd blessing lowers,
That glads the spirit of the just !
But all like Daylight's softer glances,
To shade and mantling gloom advances,
    As steps supplied to steps decline,

Slow sunset greets the Pilgrim's eyne,
Whose charms on edged horizon rove,
Like boyhood's dappled dreams of love.
Fair Day in dimming purple drest,
Gildeth her empire in the west,
As Health's half rosied tinges hid,
On faint blanched cheek of invalid.
While lightest damps of twilight kiss her,
She lingers still; we cannot miss her.
Faint seen, (with half suppress'ed sighing,)
And yet we do not see her dying.
Eftsoon with Night from fickle grey,
All that was beauteous melts away
Unphotograph'd, that friends might trace,
The dear, sweet lines that praised her face;
But Fancy left to paint her ghost,
Disgraced in Memory's jeering boast.
So on the Pilgrim's palter'd sense,
The day-beams of Omnipotence
Ere slumber'd, their effulgence bore,
"On earth to never waken more,"
For to him 'twas the scenic close
That Nature panoramic shows.

CANTO III.

I.

Life is a bond of guardian brotherhood,
    As nobly sacred as its souls doth bind;
We all at best are wanderers in a wood,
    The sport and frolic of capricious wind;
    Where 'tween hoar boughs access for light
        may find;
From whose weav'd woof may deeper shadow crowd,
    And leave shut wealth of roseate hues behind.
The blest betimes in deep of gloom are bow'd,
And their eyes catch the wave of waiting
        funeral shroud.

II.

The monk may cloister in his cell of stone,
    Or nun departed from her convent tower,
By twilight traverse river margin lone;
    Drinking close-veiled the freshness of the hour,
    Conceal chaste beauty of a virgin'd flower,
Or mountain hermit in his hut may dwell,
    And happy, trace the curse of wealth and power.
These all as ministering spirits may excel,
And earth their mute heroic figures bless:
        'tis well.

III.

But not for us on life's hot centres twirl'd,
    Far from the witching spell of chose retreat,
While tireless jars upon the hollow world,
    Tumultuous murmur of our million'd feet,
    To steal aside from where our duties meet;
And he who noblest doth his mission fill,
    Finds course with hard forbearings most replete:
Whose sea oft rough'd by the contrary will,
Needs pilot at the helm whose heart is brave
        but still.

I.

Ah! who can wander dully blind,
   That veil a spirit parch'd and dry ;
Whose languid and faint footsteps wind
   Where joyous bloom and plenty lie ?
To such, the festal tones of mirth,
That waken from the sons of earth :
The mellow light that haunting roams,
From the pure shrine of hallow'd homes,
Inspire with zeal the dearth of yearning ;
Past fled, forever unreturning,
While pours a melancholy train,
Deep drap'd in mourning's weeds of pain.
All but for him who never knew,
Anointing sunlight, balmy dew,
Nor drank with knitted friend or kin,
Affection's draught divorced of sin ;
Or he who had, for whom sole smil'd,
Once mother, wife, and infant child ;
All pass'd in Want's delirious rave,
To nameless rest of flowerless grave :
Now dead in lust, will heaven forgive ?
Vain wreck'd through all he knew to live :
The crown of growing public stamp,
Unpitying that we call a TRAMP.

II.

Along the line the Pilgrim trode,
   Whiles rustled low the shifting breeze ;
Soft as a hazy streamlet, flow'd
   Through vista of the tufted trees,
The latticed light of cottage bower,
Pale borne thro' net of vine and flower,
Where lamp is lit, perchance for maid,
Waiting in bridal robe arrayed ;
Perchance for matron o'er her sick,
Who anxious trims her nightly wick,
And harks with startled sense to hear,
The sigh that drops upon her ear.
Mayhap 'tis light in chamber'd rest,
For one sojourns a distant guest,

Who bends him by his couch to pray,
That God may bless and keep for aye.
The ploughboy late goes up the hill,
With wearied feet, reluctant will:
A dull, good-natur'd, hopeful scion,
Who stoops to pluck the dandelion,
Or break a whip from thorny hedge,
Of dusky lane and skirts its edge:
Whose lazy feet do half repine,
To cobwebb'd search the loit'ring kine:
Whose sire tired bent on busy knee,
From barn loud calls impatiently,
In tones are much too harsh for youth,
The Pilgrim deems, and foster ruth.
On further by a wicket gate,
Two seeming lovers am'rous wait,
Like cooing doves of neighboring eave,
Contented, yet that lightly grieve.
The old man in his speechless want,
Did feel as nature chose to taunt,
In gaudiest apparel drest,
To shine upon his sterile breast.
Ah me! it could but bring relief
Were he to know secluded grief.
The daylight glows while Darkness hides,
    Vocation'd solitaire below;
In noisome cell free Joy abides,
    But Sorrow veils her cheek of wo!

III.

A tottering stranger by the edge
    Of fruited orchard's crumbling wall,
Where nigh the damps of watery sedge,
    On the soft twilight melting fall,
Attracts the Pilgrim's warming glance.
As onward slow his steps advance.
He sees the trembling stranger, pause
In musing as he waits a cause:
When forth a child upshoots his head,
Down sunken late and vanish'ed,

From calamus luxuriant,
Whose arms are laden with the plant.
No doubt he is the grandsire's pet,
Whose mischief works but to forget;
Who, ere dim sight were yet quite lost
In quavering age's hoary frost,
Hid antiquated spectacles
Oft 'mong his mother's basket spools,
And, mounting from the verge of this,
Embolden'd claim'd the nightly kiss.
He imag'd fills the Pilgrim's brain,
Fond figure fair of memory's train,
The brother cherish'd of his youth,
Who fail'd in childhood's hour of ruth,
Yet lives, ay yes! in holy tears,
The soul blest star of manhood years;
To angel life and glory caught,
And he still left to face a lot,
That sullied prints the virgin snow,
With weary feet that come and go.
Now as is lifted dimpled palm,
In innocent, confiding calm,
Life's veteran joins it in embrace,
While twilight drifteth o'er his face,
And dim orb shows no light can find,
Alas! that he is wholly blind.
Fain would the Pilgrim loose his tongue,
If comfort from it could be wrung,
But grief ofttimes is sacred held,
   Like memory of the glorious dead :
And countless is the soul repell'd,
   Enliven'd lustre fain had shed.

IV

How strange along the mind's hallways,
   Impression lighted hath a guide ;
And easy, pale-companion'd strays,
   Through many an absent chamber wide.
O'er memory's room of tender muse,
Tear blind, the Pilgrim fond pursues.

He minds of one, a spirit high,
That crossed his footpath momently.
Of cultured gift, of manhood strong,
With love of right, with love of song ;
Whose ardent bosom breath'd a flame,
That time nor distance could not tame,
Nor the cold air of maiden coy,
Subdue glow'd embers or destroy.
Indeed it is a desolate thing,
To sit 'neath such o'ershadowing,
And none but God who knoweth all,
Can read what o'er the heart may fall.
Down the dark gulf of madness deep,
He fell, whose fall the angels weep ;
And in that still and awful time,
Fair life he closed—say not in crime !
O Life, whose beauty's flick'ring beam,
Came o'er me as a summer dream,
Now veil'd in gloom of earthly night,
Conceal'd from ray of Reason's light,
Thy tree is blasted to the core,
With kind to never blossom more,
Nor thy fair foliaged pendant leaf,
Wind flutter thro' the season brief ;
But harsh transplanted, and in haste,
Thy stricken bough o'er desert waste,
Must bend to shelter sickly plant,
'Mid desolation's chosen haunt.
Yet clear to Nature's sense divine,
I know but she half pours in thine,
Long falleth many a chasten'd sound,
Of heart-chord dolorous and profound,
That will not let thee be resign'd ;
To cold neglect of stranger mind,
That would perchance about thy name,
Hang cruel pall of crimson shame.
Ah me ! that I must give thee up,
Forg'd element of Sorrow's cup,
In darkness, mortal lustre dead,

From whence the light of years is fled;
But borne art thou to fitter hands,
  Where wisdom'd mercy cannot fail;
The Saviour of the world who stands,
  To soothe benighted and the frail.

V.

Then Pilgrim turn'd to one, a friend,
  Of taste refin'd, frame delicate,
Whose doom earth-skill nor aid can mend,
  Nor lift the veil o'erspreads his fate.
He had an artist's soul divine,
Than poet's doth far nobler shine.
One day along his pictur'd wall,
He led my ardent gaze, to fall
Upon a ship whose hulk alone,
The wave of sea to shore had blown.
"A wreck is this, upheav'd and dry,"
Said he, "the same, in sooth, am I."
And when the night had nestled down,
O'er fresh-mown mead and pasture brown;
Had wife and child to neighbor prest,
To yield a bed for friendship's guest;
Perchance to be beyond the reach
Unconscious, of confiding speech
Of secret, wisely better told,
Than chain'd for aye in chamber cold;
He said as how misfortune's flame,
Had wither'd and defaced his frame,
Then ruthlessly had both combin'd
To sap the germs of immortal mind.
For years his was a quiet lot,
Secluded from the common thought,
All ignorant of crafty ways,
That comes of studious nights and days.
Then came a spirit o'er his dreams,
That more than queen of mortal seems;
One that had learned forbidden craft,
And foul-dregg'd cup of wanton quaff'd:
Whose heart of guile, led guileless, free,
Relentless to captivity.

And when a heart though blunt, whose tone,
Well-meaning, whisper'd in his own,
Bespoke her character and shame,
He would not hearken, nor would blame,
Till her vile lips confirm'd the same.
Alas! for him whose child-like faith,
  In cruel man had ne'er been broken ;
But moistens with his holiest breath,
  The promise of his rainbow token ;
Till Treachery stalks across his path,
  To melt the hues by Fancy thriven :
Bann'd spirit then no comfort hath,
  But that which freely pours from heaven !

VI.

To him it was the knell of hope,
  On this broad earth forevermore ;
His life thenceforth had downward slope,
  And tiring, up no longer bore.
He heard the bells toll in the sky,
Dull lipp'd in cold monotony ;
Harsh dissonance bereft of tune,
Whose sexton's task fills not too soon.
Hot Fever laid her hand on him,
And shot a spark through every limb,
And left him humble, so that when
He trod among his fellow-men,
Reaction with reversing feet,
Sudden as blow from watchman's beat,
Might cast him prostrate, quick and hard,
Sense-veil'd, on stone or spreading sward.
The heat of summer's rays intense.
That weighs so strong on dullest sense,
O'erpow'ring left him without care,
Swoon'd subject of the sun's red glare,
One noon, when scythe in hand he thought
To turn a swath around the lot.
From this mishap of dread sunstroke,
His soul to blasted night awoke,
Awoke, but not to meekly pray ;

Too much despair'd to hope for day,
I saw him then, and pitied too,
Real nobleman of nature's due.
His friends beheld his cureless plight,
And as to gauzy film his night,
Advised that he should straightway marry,
And matrimonial tonnage carry ;
Who yielded, while they pointing clamor'd,
To jovial maid of him enamor'd.
Though wide off staid Discretion's track,
On which keen Reason oft looks back,
Such harrowing tale of heart, so true,
With veteran scars e'er fresh and new,
Unstrained, were quite enough to make
The sternly solitary, dread
The charms of woman and forsake
The pleasing thought to sometime wed.

VII.

Firesides with many a glittering light,
O'er one long league in distance shone ;
Bursting upon the Pilgrim's sight,
Apart dissevered and alone ;
Like camp-fires sentinell'd on the hill,
Whose gleamy fagot far and still,
Doth seem to pierce the midnight deep,
And sober vigil steadfast keep.
Fain had the wanderer found a bed,
Whereon to rest his weary head ;
Nor might he thus have long deplor'd
The welcome of a kindly board ;
For rustic hearts are soft design'd,
And rustic charity is kind,
But with that diffidence of pride,
To gentle modesty allied,
He paused each time before some gate,
Then passed, forlorn, disconsolate,
Ill starr'd and with a soul imbued,
With shame of novel beggarhood.
How hard the struggle, deep the pain,

For frugal and industrious age,
Bereft by greed of lowly gain,
  Or sent adrift by children's rage
To lean on charity at last,
  Dependent, and without a copper;
With halt, the blind, demented cast,
  In dreary almshouse of the pauper!

VIII.

It soon grew late for full repose.
The hard industrious ere retires,
While farm house light no longer glows,
  Or pales to flick'ring chimney fires,
Save few that stand, like picket post,
To watch and guard the sleeping host.
The house-wife, later than the rest,
Yet lingers, by her labors press'd,
To do some drudgery, aching bows,
Some garment mend for chimney'd spouse,
(Who stolid whiffs his smoky pipe,
The pattern of a backwoods type,)
Or soil'd blouse sew for Dick, the erring,
Their child unthankful and uncaring,
Who no doubt got the horrid rent
While on some urchin mischief bent ;
In bird's-nest theft delay'd a fall,
Or usage from a playmate brawl.
Such ramblings rode the Pilgrim's mind,
Like hasting tenants of the wind.
Paus'd interval presents a face,—
A mother's, with its care and grace,
That watched his cradle while he grew ;
Long, long before he thought or knew;
Him brought through infantile mishaps,
So full of netted wiles and traps :
That nurs'd the sickness of his youth
And taught him gentleness and truth.
He sees her now of fragile build,
Affection-warm'd and argus will'd,
Industrious, careful, keen and mild,

Strong sens'd, not often false beguil'd
Through fondness by a child's caprice,
To be thereby deprived of peace.
To pure religion duteous wed,
But wanting much directer head.
In features plain, in manners fit,
Where care and age do lightly sit;
A being either sex doth honor,
And good will genuine crowd upon her,
A soul that long hath conscious sway'd
    Each nobler impulse of the bosom,
Uprooted virile vices laid
    And in their stead bade virtues blossom ;
Whose spirit dwelleth with our weal,
    Alway invested with its care on ;
Whose soothing touch we yearn to feel
    When partial Earth grows cold and barren !

IX.

Anon a dark and sombre wood
    Uprose on either side the path,
So dense in sunless solitude
    Pale sward could know not aftermath.
'Twas monarch realm of pine and birch
Where wild-bird makes its evening perch
And spreads aside a sort of walk
Where pigeons roost in wondrous flock.
The screech-owl from a stub's dead height
Halloos along the dismal night,
While whipporwill's sad warblings float
Melodious from her plaintive throat.
This is the deep, secluded grove
She nightly haunting seems to love.
The old man half possess'd with fear,
In trepidation journeys here.
The jack-o'-lantern's mass of light
Slow stealeth as it were, to fright,
Where low, perchance, some dead man lies,
That, wrapt in horror, clos'd his eyes—
The victim of the robber bold,

Who gash'd his throat and hid for gold.
The dark is taught to terror's brood
And evils veil beneath her hood,
That will not bear the face of day,
But then dissolve like mist away.
The grandam tells of wooded sprites,
Or water-wraiths beheld o' nights,
Of foster boy was whilom lost,
Nor heard of more through autumn's frost.
Or storied hag, of border'd wild,
That charm'd with idle tale the child,
Whose ghosts and fairies multiplied
Till hill was peopled and woodside,
And fear rose high within the heart,
In late hour gloom to homeward start.
All their dread pictures once again
Flitted across the Pilgrim's brain,
With saved imaginary lore,
The weird and strange of later yore,
Uprose to start his half-craz'd years
With shape or sound of phantom fears.
A soft wind through the branches stealing,
Mute, mournfully impress'd a feeling
Of utter loneliness and gloom,
Devout subaltern of the tomb.
Through hoar-moss'd tree trunks, feebly nurs'd,
A light on raptur'd Pilgrim burst.
He follow'd where the welcome bore,
As ship that seeks fraternal shore,
And shortly squalid cabin found
Where woodman's axe had clear'd the ground.
Most like that some one sick were there,
Who needed nurse to watch and care.
The Pilgrim had but few steps more,
To reach and rap at entrance door,
When bursting hound loud bellowing near'd ;
In sudden fright he disappear'd.
The dwelling's inmates thought, no doubt,
Some night marauder prowl'd about,

And watch-dog set upon his track,
He bravely turn'd whelp howling back.
The home that aims bereft to be
Of stranger hospitality,
Hath but to win of mongrel breed,
 A whining puppy, cross'd to bite,
Can chase pedestrian o'er the mead,
 Or down the road till out of sight.

X.

The hoar wood pales upon the eyne,
 For wilderness perplex and gray,
Whose meshes intricate combine
 To tole unwonted steps astray.
The stars of twinkling arch were beaming,
And their far lights stood fondly streaming,
Each from its individual throne,
In set tranquillity alone,
Like watchers for the dead set free,
Or those not dead that soon may be.
He wanders on where osiers dank
Do pleasant line the velvet bank ;
Where dearth of matted foliage shows,
Fair sheet of water shimmering glows,
Whose wave, pellucid, deep and wide,
Doth skirt the solitude to glide.
He drops him down on knoll'ed height,
A-wearied and exhaused quite,
That high o'erlooks the moonlit stream,
Where myriad shapes reflected seem.
He thinks how he, undaunted here,
Might seek and find a watery bier.
How cool the depths that lie below,
And murmurs breathe to murm'ring wo,
That nigh the sedgy grasses lave,
As half to woo him to their grave !
And then of Fate, how dark she flies,
And left hath none to close his eyes.
He feels to drift his form might float
Unseen by fisher's dancing boat,

Unrecked his corse, unborne from hence,
Would seek again her elements.
Though thousands take the fatal leap
For suicide's untimely sleep.
The host know not by dread deterr'd,
Unwhisper'd the confession'd word.
When ashen hues the cheek of Death,
We would not shy like anch'ret rover,
But court warm pulse of kindred breath
Till Shadowy Valley's chill be over.

XI.

Upspringing Pilgrim, agile stept
Like one who treads with fearful care,
In dim cathedral's high transept
The holy frankincense to bear ;
Like woman's arm in peril's hour
Nerv'd as by supernatural power,
His footsteps firm to distance tread
From where wile Danger's snare is spread.
Far fades he in the wilderness
Where dim-seen cavernous recess,
Unlantern'd, opes its grinning jaws,
Nor stirs the welcome throb to pause.
He presses on 'till failing breath
Prostrates upon the barren heath,
Where doubly cold the objects rise
Even to unexpecting eyes !
On the hard turf he lieth now,
Beside a rock's projecting brow :
A rock, save but to lichens bare,
The centuries shap'd and laid it there.
Two springs from out its base distil,
And thread in streamlet down the hill.
A vulture crowns the neighboring stub,
Where lowlier spreads dwarf stunted shrub.
Too bleak the soil for warmth of flowers,
Unseen to grace the desert hours.
Hard by in clump of stricken bushes,
Ere Dawn the face of morning flushes,

The red fox seeks his stony den,
From pilfers nigh the haunts of men,
And barks to pierce the cave below
At trespass of the stranger foe.

XII.

Where this secluded spot of land,
In hoary stillness seem'd to stand,
In thought he lay till balmy sleep
Did o'er his tired limbs deign to creep,
And made mute memory of his wo,
Forget to start from cheek aglow.
Ay! what a glorious thing to rest
And have of calmest dreams the best;
Though when the rosy morn awakes
Their hue from red to dark partakes!
The heart with joy ought overflow,
Save in the gloom of guilty wo.
How oft immur'd in prison cell
The captive's closing hours might tell:
Hours with a gallows on the morn,
With shame for her who saw him born,
Were passed in many a glorious dream
That could not false or flitting seem.
And as there couch'd in twilight grey,
O'erwearied Pilgrim mutely lay,
A smile uplit his furrow'd face,
Late charge of sorrow's cold embrace,
And would to those who gaze have told,
Reflex of transport they behold.

XIII.

Our varied mind is limitless
As space remotest planets press,
And when we only peer askance
Upon the languag'd countenance,
What depth of gloom or pregnant bliss
We mark and yet we lightly miss.
We view a bounded world confin'd
Within this wondrous stretch of mind,
And too of habitable distress,

That sages know of but to guess,
Awakes, expands. contracts, repines,
And dies, unleft of trailing signs ;
Like perturb'd stir of windy wave,
That ruffles but to screen its grave.
Thus half the griefs that mortals feel
They deem unmeet to e'er reveal.
The aged man's limbs wax stiff and cold ;
A mist hath spread his vestments old,
As in the night-air, dense and chill,
He lies so pale, and calm, and still.
But vision-wrapt he knows it not,
While deep entranc'd in pleasing thought,
Unbridl'd Fancy gaily soars
And to the Pilgrim's heart restores
A loftier joy than could illume
His pathway in its sunniest bloom ;
And yet, though sweeter than the earth,
Or grandest gift of creature birth,
This fancy pulse, electric given,
Is only lightest touch of heaven.

XIV.

The soul uplifts o'er earthy clod,
   And quits this lowly vale of tears,
For heaven's enamell'd pastures broad,
   To visit her eternal years.
She sees the dwellers throng'ed press,
Array'd in light of snowy dress,
And pines to be among them number'd,
But somehow conscious seems encumber'd.
They strike their harps with glad refrain,
And music flows in charm'ed strain,
The raptur'd wish that nought would sever,
To which the earth's is discord ever.
Then mute prelude those harps of glory,
   That melt among departed things ;
And sav'd for record parchments hoary,
   Impond'rous tracery of their wings.
Now blend in chorus all their voices

To melody of perfect strain,
While every spirit glad rejoices,
　High o'er the fleshly thrall of pain.
Joy but to trait'ress, ill behavior,
To praise Creator and the Saviour;
To chant in sanctuaried leisure
Delightful psalms of holy measure!

I.

" To great Redeemer praising,
　Thrill our hearts with holiest flame ;
Supreme, love's altar raising,
　Blest we float IIis lisp'ed name.
Whose mercy, undeceiving,
　Bears us while for aye ascend
Glad hymns of glad thanksgiving,
　Soft as tints harmonious blend.

II.

"IIis love to us is boundless
　And enlargeth everywhere,
A Nature thus whole soundless,
　So to manifest a care,
Hath meed of praise unceasing
　While the timeless centuries roll ;
Meek parting, fond releasing,
　From the proud clime of the soul !

III.

" Let not in zeal devoted,
　Tongue to dying silence fall,
While endless cycles noted,
　To unending cycles call ;
But in restraintless union,
　Merg'd with blessing more and more,
Chaunt all in high communion
　Hymns to God whom we adore !"

XV.

'Twas thus in bliss the myriads spirits,
　Loud sang with fervent souls aflame;
'Tis thus must each who heaven inherits,
　Free'd from veil'd sorrow, chant the same.

All clearly sketch'd was the Elysium
That fram'd the old man's tranquil vision,
In mazy wilderness and night,
Born of the freshest hues and bright.
'Twas beautiful, ah! yes, and tender,
And link'd with melting gleam of splendor;
Far holier than the things we trace
With touches of divinest grace!
Such beauteous fancies vanish soon ;
They cannot blend with life's harsh tune :
They melt and flow from out the heart,
Or with it companied depart.
And for the Pilgrim who had won
Fair images from colors dun,
Fate look'd with smile, serene and kind,
And bade him be with Death resign'd.
For lo! as clos'd the dreamy spell
That wide in folds of blessing fell,
The spirit took her heavenward flight,
Upward o'er dropping dews of blight,
Whither his thoughts were bent to soar,
Where now they'll rise forevermore!

I.

O! why do we live in the terror of death ?
Why dread it like canker of poisonous breath ?
Why steadfastly cling we with resolute will
To mingle and mourn with th' universe still,
When messenger waits us, with comforting hand,
To lead his sad children to sorrowless land ?

II.

There kindred unnumber'd repos'd with the dead,
From thousand stern trials eternal are fled ;
Who wait while they yearn on the far-distant shore,
Till joined in the pleasure of meeting once more ;
There never to part like a wind-shaken leaf ;
There never to lie on the bosom of Grief.

III.

No sorrow can float to that bless'ed abode ;
No law hath upbuilded on fallible code ;

No fiends with their enginery massacre man ;
No dark dread of martyr dissembles its plan ;
But Peace, Love and Beauty, in emulous reign,
Sway sceptre unsullied o'er boundless domain.

IV.

'Tis fiat of nature, our natures to shun
The dark, gloomy path of the Terrible One ;
Whatever of trust in the bosom may dwell,
When bid we to scenes that delighted farewell ;
And none but with crush'd heart that knows but to
        sigh,
Unseen in the cold shade of marble would lie !

XVI.

No friend the mendicant was near
To drop for love's dear pledge a tear ;
His limbs to smoothly press, or close
His eyelids as in eve repose.
But o'er his slumbers, still and fast,
Had pale horse pangless breathing pass'd.
Low bound in trance by Nature's jar
His uncag'd spirit dash'd afar.
Not thus are myriads usher'd free
When death discumbers tenantry,
Though crown'd by gold, or breath of fame,
That fans to careless ears a name ;
Who harbor faith in this dread hour,
That quakes to face a righteous power ;
Whose vain loss high as warnings play,
In toys old Time must toss away.
If Justice held her lamp of light
We would not grope in rayless night.
True worth to pomp with glittering ties
Sinks lowly in this age's eyes.

XVII.

Night fled away, and morning's dawn
In tranquil quietude led on,
While from the east horizon, came
The beaming sun's reflected flame,
And from his Oriental car,

He cheer'd this solitude afar;
E'en this secluded glen where lay,
The old man turn'd to pallid clay.
The sighing winds his requiem bore,
Along the river's pebbly shore;
The waste took up the pensive strain,
And hied it far toward bosom'd main.
But Nature soon her grief did sate,
And ceas'd to moan, bewail his fate.
The buzzard in his hunger came,
And feasted on his fetid frame,
So quickly fallen to decay,
But wakes his soul to endless day.
To rest at last he wing'd his flight,
For o'er is Pilgrimage of Light.
And such it was, O joy! for lo,
Light ray'd the closing hour of wo!
The traveller caught in humid shower,
That soon discovers sunny hour,
Forgets the watery drench that dries,
In singing brooks and laughing skies.
The mother whom her babe doth bear,
Though robb'd by many a night of care,
When manhood's flush looms brave and tall.
Her woman's pride forgets it all.
Ah! o'er us each the night must droop,
In wild, or cot, or ocean sloop;
And while wide contrast deftly glows
Round hearts that press to last repose,
Each is alike of fleeting breath,
Fram'd in the common mould of death.
All things to us, the real or hop'd,
Vague sink at last untelescop'd.
And, musing in this borrow'd light,
To him who doth these lines indite,
There comes that holy spell of peace
And melody can never cease.

ɪ.

Lovely visions steal o'er me and dance on my sight

In their beautiful halos of lustre and light,
And they waft me afar on the pinions of bliss
To a clime that is balmy and pleasant I wis,
And the hours as they flit in their fleetness away
Lend no forerunner token of fugitive day ;
And untrumpeted forth from my presence depart
All the pictures that glow'd on the pulse of my heart,
While a breeze stirs each leaflet of forested brown,
Till a sun-tinted shower pats tumultuously down.
Though the spirit of mystery veileth my soul,
Yet it cannot be hid in the light of its goal.

II.

As the shadows of night-fall hang o'er the hush'd
world
Like the disk of an orb o'er a mild planet's face,
Do I muse in the twilight where peace is soft curl'd
And hoar solitude shelters in nestled embrace,
And I hear on the night-wind that journeys abroad
Through the woodland serene and the thicket untrod,
Nigh the door of the musal one's solitaire grot,
The diversified music of audible thought.
And I ask in my heart why I linger unblest
When a world of affection lies cold and at rest.
Though the spirit of mystery veileth my soul,
Yet it can not be hid in the light of its goal.

III.

Fills there aught that is fair or there aught which is
good,
That is strewn like the leaf in the autumnal wood ?
Glitters gem that we wish, jewell'd costly and rare ?
Wonted flow'ret with perfume for all the wide air ?
Do we gain the fond treasures that dearest we prize,
When we lag in the seekings that ravish our eyes ?
Ah ! they dwell in a difficult climate apart,
From the world that is rife and whole tax they the
heart,
And drap'd years may trail by ere they come to be
ours,
And e'en then they may wither like garlanded flowers.

Though the spirit of mystery veileth my soul,
Yet it can not be hid in the light of its goal.

IV.

Let the tempest low bow in the rush of its might;
Let it ride the fleet blast like a spectre of night:
Let it mantle my form in the shadow of fears,
And besprinkle my soul with the essence of tears :
Let meek sunshine descend through its atmosphere
     warm,
To beguile the dark hours by a wizard-lit charm.
I will lean on the strength of the Merciful One,
Who will rock me to sleep when my trials are done,
And will bless as is meet though He oft may deny,
That the querulous question vehemently why.
Though the spirit of mystery veileth my soul,
Yet it can not be hid in the light of its goal.

V.

I'll uprise with a zeal all alive to the task,
That affection may prompt, or that duty may ask ;
And will pay lowly court for the blessings of earth,
And the graces of virtue auspicious in worth.
I will gaze on the lighted tower beacon of Love,
Must imparadise hearts way directed Above.
And though hope should grow languid in weary
     desire,
And my sacrific'd bosom be reav'd of her fire,
Even then in the deep of Night's tremulous stream
Would I lave, for hope's love floweth boundless I
     deem.
Though the spirit of mystery veileth my soul,
Yet it can not be hid in the light of its goal.

www.ingramcontent.com/pod-product-compliance
Lightning Source LLC
Chambersburg PA
CBHW031245260626
47169CB00007B/2451